I am the
property of:

write your name here

✓

_____

_____

_____

For Mum and Dad ~JS

For Glen P ~TW

Little Tiger Press

1 The Coda Centre, 189 Munster Road, London SW6 6AW

www.littletigerpress.com

First published in Great Britain 1996

This edition published 2012

Text copyright © Julie Sykes 1996, 2012

Illustrations copyright © Tim Warnes 1996, 2012

Julie Sykes and Tim Warnes have asserted their rights

to be identified as the author and Illustrator of this

work under the Copyright, Designs and Patents Act, 1988

Printed in China

ISBN 978 1 84895 465 6

LTP 1400/0393/0412

10 9 8 7 6 5 4 3 2 1

I Don't Want to go to Bed!

Julie Sykes   Tim Warnes

Little Tiger Press

London

Little Tiger did not like going to bed.
Every night when Mummy Tiger said,
"Bedtime!" Little Tiger would say,

"But I don't want
to go to bed!"

One night when Little Tiger said, "I don't want to go to bed!" Mummy roared, "All right, you can stay up all night!" So Little Tiger scampered off into the jungle.

Little Tiger went to visit his best friend, who was having his ears washed.

"Why are you still up?" growled
Daddy Lion.
"I dont want to go to bed!"
said Little Tiger. And he ran off
before Daddy Lion could wash
his ears too!

Little Tiger went to visit
Little Elephant.
"Why are you still up?" trumpeted Mummy.
"I don't want to go to bed!"
said Little Tiger, and he b o u n c e d
off before Mummy Elephant could
put him to bed, too!

Little Monkey was already fast asleep.

"Why are you still up?" whispered Mummy Monkey.

"I dont want to go to bed!" Little Tiger whispered back. And he tiptoed off before Mummy Monkey made him fall asleep, too!

Suddenly it seemed very dark.
Little Tiger didn't know where to
go next. It was the first time
he had been in the jungle so late.

Little Tiger looked
up and saw. . .

...two very large yellow eyes staring back at him!

It was a bush baby.
"Shouldn't you be in bed?"
she asked.
"I don't want to
go to bed!"
said Little Tiger
shivering.

"Let's take you home," said Bush Baby.
"Your mummy will be worried about you."
"I don't want to go home!"
said Little Tiger.
But he didn't want to be left alone
in the dark either.

So he followed Bush Baby through the jungle.

"Ah, there you are!" said Mummy Tiger.

"I don't want to go to..." yawned Little Tiger, and he fell fast asleep! Mummy Tiger tucked him up and turned to Bush Baby...

...but Bush Baby had disappeared into the jungle before Mummy Tiger could tuck her up, too!

Exciting new reads
from Little Tiger Press!

For information regarding any of the above titles or for our catalogue, please contact us:

Little Tiger Press, 1 The Coda Centre, 189 Munster Road, London SW6 6AW

Tel: 020 7385 6333 · Fax: 020 7385 7333 · E-mail: info@littletiger.co.uk · www.littletigerpress.com